Amie.

One of my favs! ♡

VERY WICKED BEGINNINGS

A BRIARCREST ACADEMY PREQUEL NOVELLA

Ilsa Madden-Mills xoxo

ILSA MADDEN-MILLS

This is a work of fiction. Names, characters, places, brands, media, and incidents are either the product of the author's imagination or are used fictitiously. The author acknowledges the trademarked status and trademark owners of various products referenced in this work of fiction, which have been used without permission. The publication/use of these trademarks is not authorized, associated with, or sponsored by the trademark owners.

Cover Photography by Toski Covey Photography
Cover Design by Sommer Stein of Perfect Pear Designs
Cover Model Tanner Belcher
Editing by Rachel Skinner of Romance Refined
Formatting by JT Formatting

www.ilsamaddenmills.com

Printed in the United States of America

First Edition: May 2014
Library of Congress Cataloging-in-Publication Data

Madden-Mills, Ilsa
Very Wicked Beginnings (A Briarcrest Academy Prequel Novella) – 1st ed
ISBN-13: 978-0990368434

1.Very Wicked Beginnings—Fiction. 2.Fiction—Romance
3.Fiction—Contemporary Romance 4. Fiction—Novella

LITTLE DOVE
PUBLISHING

For those of you who have ever lost anything, whether it's simply your keys or something as heartbreaking as your mind.

For my husband, the best beta reader a girl could have.
You're my Viking, for reals, babe.
I love you.

Welcome
to
Briarcrest Academy

CUBA

"Two things about me: I play football—and girls."
–Cuba

September
Junior Year

I WANTED THE gorgeous girl in the window.

More specifically, I wanted the dark-haired girl dancing inside the Symthe Arts Building as I stood outside on the twenty-yard line at football practice, fixated on her when I should have been focused on the line of scrimmage. I adjusted my helmet and squinted through the afternoon Dallas sun.

Did I know her?

Movement from other players on the field pulled me back. Good thing. As defensive end, it was my job to put the screws to or sack the quarterback as soon as the ball snapped.

Clearly, I was off today. Probably because I had a shit ton of homework waiting on me at home. With my dreams of being a doctor someday, I took each assignment seriously at Briarcrest Academy, planning for the future.

Just like every seventeen-year-old kid out there, I had the usual stresses.

But I did have more than the average. I had a sick mom.

Those thoughts faded when I looked back at the window and watched the girl run and then leap in the air, her body doing some kind of crazy in-the-air-leg-split-thing. *Damn*. She'd gotten at least four feet off the ground.

Then, after landing on her feet light as a feather, she danced away from my view. I waited for her to come back, wanting to check out her toned muscles again, especially her tight ass. And then I randomly wondered if her tits were small. Weren't all dancers? Yeah. But still, she looked—

"Pay attention, Hudson!" Coach Howe yelled at me.

Fuck. Caught.

I automatically stiffened and tightened my defensive stance, running my eyes across the offensive line, waiting for the play. But Matt, the quarterback, was pussy-footing around, still undecided if they were gonna run or pass.

I got bored.

Out of my peripheral vision, I caught a flash of pink dashing past the window.

She was back.

And like I was addicted to her, my eyes drifted to the building again, one part baffled by the fascination, the other part wanting to get another glimpse of her long legs. As I watched, she adjusted her ponytail as she laughed up at her ballet partner—who was a dude. *Crazzzy*. Yeah, you'd think he'd be all feminine and shit, but he wasn't. Nope.

Dude looked buff, like he could bench press a school bus.

Something about the girl had me riveted. It was probably that short skirt she wore. I pictured slipping my hand underneath it to her panties. Her core would be hot, on fire for me, of course, and I'd ease my finger inside her wet—

Bam! I took a hard hit from Tank Carson, an All District offensive guard I routinely ran circles around in practice. He might be big, but I was quick and smart and had more moves than a freaking octopus. So the chance to plant my distracted ass on the turf was an early Christmas present for him. That's what I get for letting some piece of ass get in my game, even if it was practice.

And so. My unprepared body flew through the air with 290 pounds of Tank on top of it. My head hit the turf, the contact reverberating inside my helmet and then everything went black …

A few minutes later, I blinked up into the hot sun, stretched out on a bench alongside the field. One of the assistant coaches gave me a smirk as he leaned over and peered at my eyes.

"Ah, so you are alive."

I nodded, wincing as I sat up.

"Any nausea?" he asked, handing me a Gatorade and a bottle of Aleve.

I took both and shook my head. I'd had worse hits.

"Just woozy. Didn't see him coming is all." How fucking embarrassing.

He watched me swallow down two pills. "You got mowed down because you weren't paying attention. Don't be pulling that shit during a game. You thinking of getting a football scholarship next year?"

I rubbed my temple and sighed. Not really. Being a

doctor seemed more important, but I didn't say that. And sure I loved football, but ultimately, my goal in life was to help people, to make up for all the bad shit I did four years ago.

Still, there was a ton of pressure on the team. And I wanted to be a leader, someone the other players looked up to. Especially since the quarterback was a jerk, all into making himself look good.

"Sorry, Coach. I got distracted. It won't happen again."

He slapped me on the back. "Your eyes are good, and there's no swelling. It's possible you have a very mild concussion, so the best thing to do is rest up. I called your dad to come check you out."

I said okay and after he walked away, I glanced over to see if the strange object of my stupidity was still in the window. I didn't see her, and the studio lights looked dimmed, so I guessed her practice had ended pretty much as soon as I'd taken the hit.

Now, I'd never know who she was.

I hadn't gotten a good look at the details of her face. Sure, I knew her hair was dark and her body tight, but that was about it. Put her in regular clothes, and she'd fit right in with half the girls at Briarcrest.

I got a pang of disappointment at not knowing her name, and it surprised me.

Why did I care about some girl in the window anyway?

I had plenty of other girls, probably prettier, to keep me occupied. And I didn't dig chasing girls. I liked immediate gratification when it came to the opposite sex, and if I had to work too hard for it, then it usually wasn't worth my time.

Yet still my thoughts persisted.

Had she seen me looking? Did she know who I was?

Because face it, everyone did.

Obviously she was a student at BA, but if I didn't know her, it told me right away she didn't hang in my social circle. In other words, she wasn't popular. *Meh.* Everyone here thinks I'm the king of the school, even calling me Hollywood because they think my life is golden and perfect.

But it isn't.

Because no matter who people think you are, no one really knows what's underneath. The real truth is I'm an irresponsible, self-centered fuck who puts his own needs before others.

Just ask my mother. I've let her down plenty of times.

LATER THAT NIGHT at home, I relaxed in bed, finishing up some homework for Honors Chemistry.

Dad poked his head through the doorway. Earlier, he'd picked me up from school and taken me to the physician's office where I'd gotten the okay that all was well. Since then, we'd eaten a light dinner and watched some television together. Typical evening at our house.

He eased in the room, adjusting his wire-framed glasses. "Hey, I gotta run out for a late staff meeting with the team." He owns part of the Dallas Mavericks, like a big part. "You gonna be okay to check in on your mom in a few? Make sure she's good?"

At the mention of her name, I got tense. Sighing, I eased out of bed. "Yeah, sure. She sleeping?"

I had no idea what her evening had consisted of since she hadn't come down for dinner. She did that a lot, stayed in her room to read or watch mindless television. I don't know what the difference was between watching it alone or with us but apparently there was.

He rubbed his jaw, wearing a thoughtful expression. "She seems good. No need to rush or worry, okay?" He checked his watch. "I'll be home around midnight."

I nodded and watched him walk down the hall, wishing I could leave too. That I could get in my Porsche and drive all the way out of Dallas, away from all the darkness that permeated my existence here in Highland Park.

Because much like my mother, I was alive but barely living.

A couple of hours later, I finished my homework and went upstairs to her room. As the door creaked open, my mouth got dry, wondering if maybe I should have come in sooner to see her, but that was stupid.

She'd said she wouldn't try to kill herself again. She'd promised me.

I eased over to her bed and found her safe and sound, lying curled up like a little girl. Long dark hair cascaded across her pillow and rested against honey-colored skin. My mother was Brazilian and beautiful—everyone said so. She'd met and married my father while they'd both been students at Baylor University, both of them in the business department. He had light brown hair with pale skin and freckles while she was petite and exotic. They were opposites in personality too. He was gregarious and fun and loved to talk. She, well, wasn't. Not anymore.

He loved to tell the story of how they met. About how he fell in love with her as soon as she walked into his dorm room on his buddy's arm. Yeah, my dad loved her so much he stole his friend's girl. Oh, he'd had to work for it because apparently she'd played hard to get, but he'd eventually won her over with his charming personality and relentless pursuit. His motto was *all's fair in love when a drop-dead gorgeous Brazilian is involved.* I smiled, picturing him wooing my mom. Begging her to go to dinner with him. Asking her to marry him.

That had been nearly twenty years ago, though, and now they didn't even share the same bed. And I don't think it was dad's choice. I'd watch him look at her sometimes. Like she hung the fucking moon. Like she was his star in the sky. But she never gazed at him. Or me.

I leaned down and moved a wayward curl, brushing my lips against her cheek. She smelled good, and dammit if it didn't make my whole body draw up in pain, remembering a time when she'd hug me and tell me she loved me. Rubbing my aching chest, I took a step back, putting distance between us, wanting to run out of that room.

Not wanting to face the reality of her sickness.

I just missed her. I missed her singing along with a song on the radio; I missed her coming to my football games; I missed the way we used to be.

But I got it. I understood. She was hurting, slouching around the house with this hopeless look on her face. And that expression paralyzed me, yet ripped me up inside. Because she was withering away right in front of us, and no matter what we said or did, she refused to come out of it.

Her diagnosis was severe depression. Not cancer. Not even close. Physically, I guess she was healthy, if you overlooked the twenty pounds she'd put on in the past four years.

She stirred, and I took another step closer to the door. I didn't want her eyes to search the room and find mine. Because I knew what I'd see … blame. The same thing I saw every day when I looked at myself in the mirror.

Because her sickness was all my fault.

I HEADED BACK to my room for a shower.

As I stripped off my track pants and shirt, I checked out the tattoo Dad had taken me to get for my birthday this past year, the first of many tats I planned to get. This one was a long vine of twisting red roses, resting on my upper arm and curving back on my shoulder. Most of the roses were in full bloom while one—a black one—was closed up, a circle of thorns protecting it. I'd gotten that flower for my sister, Cara. I flexed my heavy bicep muscles, watching the flowers move around on my skin.

Like that dark bloom, Cara was dead. She'd been gone for four years, but not a day went by that I didn't think of her snaggle-toothed smile and strawberry-scented hair. She'd been born eight years after me, a surprise baby. A tiny replica of my mother, she'd been adored by everyone.

And at that thought, a slice of pain cut into me, and I nearly doubled over on the sink. Shit, what a fuck-up I was.

Must not think about her, I told myself.

So I thought about Ballet Girl.

I cranked up my radio and got in the shower. Before the water was even warm, I spread my legs and wrapped a hand around my cock, picturing her again, dancing, only this time I was the only one in the room with her. In my head, I stood behind her and watched her perform. My fantasy got hotter as she swayed and twirled like a beautiful goddess sent from the heavens to entertain me, looking ethereal and too damn perfect for this messed up world. I imagined her turning and seeing me and smiling so big I nearly lost my breath. *Because she knew me*. In this fantasy world, we'd been dating for a while now, spending time together, going out to dinner, laughing and talking, making out. She was in love with me and wanted me like she'd never wanted anyone or anything in her entire life. She couldn't breathe without me. She wanted to make my life *better*. And I felt the same. I'd never been in love before, but maybe this time, with her—

Whoa.

Yeah, that kind of thinking made me stop my back and forth, but then I kicked it in again, stroking myself faster and harder. She was too good to *not* dream about. I got raunchier in my head, imagining me pulling her into my arms and kissing her, our mouths wide open, tongues licking, teeth biting. Then, I got down on my knees and unlaced her sexy ballet shoes. I worked my way up and slipped my hands underneath her skirt and eased it and her panties down her long legs. She spread her legs and begged me to lick her core, and I did, tasting her for the first time. I moaned into her, my tongue finding every secret crevice, devouring her. She came, her hands fisted in my hair, her cries echoing out into the empty dance studio.

She wanted me to fuck her, her hands urging me up

off the ground, to finish what we'd started. I had to give her what she wanted. Because I wanted her more than I'd ever wanted any girl.

With furious need, I rose up and bent her over the pole that ran the length of the studio wall and took her from behind, my hands on her breasts, holding her hot skin against me. Of course, initially, I pictured her breasts as huge, but then I scaled them back, wanting to imagine her as she really was. And then suddenly I didn't want her from behind. I wanted to see her face and gaze into her eyes, even though I didn't really know what she looked like. And that frustrated me. Because this fantasy felt different, in a good way, and she seemed special—*shit, this is crazy*, I thought.

But I couldn't stop. I didn't want to. I gritted my teeth, tossing my head back into the spray of water, picturing me taking her, sinking into her softness, making her all mine. She took my pounding, crying out my name and clenching around me as she came hard. Again.

A guttural groan came deep from within me.

Fuck yeah … pumping, pumping.

And then I got dizzy in the best kind of way, feeling tingles and goose bumps as the heat built and rose until *bam!* My orgasm slammed into me, and I came for what seemed like forever, my legs giving out as I sank down to the floor of the marble tiled shower on my knees. My entire body quivered, shaking with the aftershocks. With unsteady hands, I pushed wet hair off my face.

Fuck, me.

I wanted that girl in the window.

But not enough to find her.

Dovey

"Two things about me:
I dance and I dance."
–Dovey

"ARMS UP, DOVEY," Mr. Keller, my instructor, called to me as I focused on my partner, Jacques, and the contemporary piece called *Song of the Earth* we were doing. He and I had the lead role for our annual school production, and it was a prime spot, one that would shine on my application to a ballet company next year. I needed to ace this part because I didn't have a back-up plan. Ballet was it for me.

I put my arms in the air, rounding them out in fifth position. He nodded his approval.

I continued, executing the abstract movements, some of which were more demanding than classical ballet, requiring deep *pliés* and distorted yet elegant lines. Climactic and passionate, I let myself fly as I danced the last scene, envisioning myself as the character that loses the love of her life.

Then something weird happened.

Right in the middle of my *grand jeté* tingles skipped up my spine and spread over my body. I landed and let out a shiver. It felt like someone was watching me, and I didn't mean the teacher or Jacques or one of the other dancers. The sensation was more intense, darker, making me self-conscious as I finished up my routine.

As soon as my part was done, I went off to a corner to grab a drink of water, passing by the big window that faced the west and looked out over the football practice field.

I stopped in my tracks.

A big football player was facing me on the twenty yard line, dressed in tight white football pants and a navy blue jersey. He was tall, probably a few inches over six feet, and his shoulders were impossibly broad. No clue who he was with the helmet on, but his practice jersey said number 89, yet even that meant nothing to me. I knew nada about the game or the players on the team. Well, I knew some of the players' reputations. Most were uber-rich and super popular. I mean, this was Texas where football players—especially those with looks and money— were treated like gods.

I cocked my head. Why would he stare into the dance window, and why—*slam!* He got pummeled hard by another player. I flinched and gasped, wondering if I should run out there and check on him, but then the coach loped across the field. He took the player's helmet off, but from my angle I still couldn't make out the fallen player's face. After a few minutes, he stumbled to his feet with the aid of a couple of players, and they walked him off the field and back to the sidelines.

"Dovey, you're up next," one of the other dancers said.

I glided back to the center spot, forgetting about the player.

I'm sure he wasn't looking at me anyway.

No one at BA ever sees the scholarship girl from Ratcliffe.

AFTER PRACTICE, I left the dance building to meet Spider, my bestie, in the school parking lot. Well, to be honest, I was meeting him and his random flavor of the month. Becca, maybe? Who knew. I couldn't keep up with the names considering the constant rotation he ran.

As I came around the corner of the building, I saw he had this week's girl backed up against the side of his Range Rover, his hands on her ass, all cozy as they made out. I noticed he'd colored his hair again; it was azure blue, and I had to admit, it looked good.

I paused and watched in a clinical kind of way, wondering what all the fuss was about with him. I mean, who'd ever want to kiss Spider? His mouth had been everywhere. I laughed low enough so they wouldn't hear me, still taking it all in, planning on critiquing him later on his tongue technique.

He stuck his hand up her red shirt, going for boobs, and my brows hit the roof. It wasn't even dark yet. Not that that had ever stopped him.

The girl moaned, her hands cupping his nape, her fingers caressing the hand-sized black widow tattoo he had on his neck. He pulled her closer and pumped his hips against hers.

"Spider," she moaned, picking up a leg and wrapping it around his waist.

Good grief. They were about to make their own porn movie.

I coughed.

They didn't move, their hands getting more frenzied, their kiss more heated.

"Yeah, baby, like that," Spider said gutturally as the girl put her hands in his pants.

Okay, enough. This was gross.

I put my hands up to my mouth and let out a long, shrill whistle. I grinned when Spider flinched and shot me an irritated glare. I shrugged. So. I loved to give him a hard time.

The girl straightened her shirt, her beady green eyes on me. Pissy? Most definitely.

"Bloody fucking hell. Could you have let us finish?" he said, pushing down on the giant hard-on in his jeans. His British always came out more when he was pissed, which made me smile.

I cocked a hip. "You said we were going to Portia's for a pastry, so I'm here. Jonesing for a donut, if you wanna know. If you wanted to mess around, you shoulda got a room. Or at least gotten in the car. It's right there."

The girl gave me a weird look. "You're going with us?"

"Am I?" I asked Spider, arching my brow. He'd better say yes. We'd made plans at lunch and if he bailed on me …

He gave the girl a quick peck on the mouth. "Yep. She goes with me."

Suck it, I wanted to say to her, but I just stood there,

because I'd still be here tomorrow … and her? Not so much.

I moved in closer and stuck my hand out to the girl, offering an olive branch. "Dovey Beckham. And you don't have to worry. Spider and I are just friends." I smiled, because really, *we were just friends*, and it would be nice to have a friend who was a girl.

But she gave me a look loaded with disdain. Typical reception from the rich girls who considered a girl from the projects beneath them. But maybe because Spider was watching, she put her hand out too. "Becca Mitchell. Spider's girlfriend."

I blinked to stop my eyes from rolling. She wished. Along with several others.

Then, I shot him a look to see if he agreed with that statement, but his face was a cool mask. As usual. No one could ever tell what he was thinking. But my gut sensed this girl was just passing through. Just yesterday, he'd told me about messing around with some cheerleader out at the barn, an old building that sat at the end of BA's campus and was part of the equestrian program here.

I smiled brightly back at Becca, just as fake as she was. "Great. I hope you stay that way." I rubbed my hands together. "Now, if you two are done, I just spent three hours working my ass off, and I'd like to get my carbs for the day."

We got in Spider's car, with Becca sitting in the front seat, while I sat alone in the back. Whatever.

Being alone didn't matter.

And I had secrets anyway. And that meant keeping my distance when it came to relationships, because if these spoiled rich kids knew my true story, my entire future would be over.

CUBA

"I blame myself for a lot of things.
Loving her wasn't one of them."
–Cuba

SEPTEMBER DRIFTED PAST. I went to school, played football, and partied as usual, picking a new girl to be with every Friday night after the game. I had my choice, being constantly bombarded with offers and texts and sexual innuendoes. Once I'd even hooked up with one of the teacher interns here. Fresh from the university, she'd been impressed with my athletic build, and I'd been impressed with her willingness to do anything I asked. But I was smart when it came to chicks. I always picked the ones who wouldn't be bothered when I moved on to someone else. That meant most nice girls were out.

I don't think I'm missing anything. I'm not a nice dude.

By mid October we'd won four straight games, and the sportscasters were calling me the best defensive end since BA had opened its esteemed doors in 1962. I accepted the praise because I needed the focus. Knowing I had something to work for kept me centered. I wanted to forget about my mother, and football helped with that. Girls did too.

As far as Ballet Girl went, I'd refused to let my gaze look for her in the window. No great loss. I told myself I'd built her up in my head; she really hadn't been all that.

"Cuba, dude, sit over here," Zero, another football jock, said to me as I entered the BA crowded gym. It was just after lunch, and we had an assembly today with a college recruiter. They came about once a month from various places, selling their universities. Today's speaker was from Princeton.

I headed to where Zero sat. His real name was Zack and not only were we teammates, but we were *kinda* friends. Like mine, his family was prominent in Highland Park. Yet, he didn't know everything about me. He didn't know what I'd done four years ago.

Truthfully, I didn't connect with anyone here, although if you asked most of them, they'd say we were good friends.

I sat down next to him.

"You been bulking up, Hollywood?" Zero was big into fitness.

I flexed an arm muscle. At six foot three inches I was already broader and taller than my dad. And I loved to work out because the burn it gave me numbed me out and made me so exhausted that by the time I got home and finished my homework, I'd crash.

Because I didn't want to think about what was going on with my family.

I nodded. "Yeah. Swimming is good too—" and those

words came to a halt as the pink swish of a skirt passed in front of me. The girl wearing the skirt plopped down in a seat directly in front of me. She also wore a grey hoodie, and her feet were stuck in a pair of knock-off Uggs. Pale pink tights were on her legs.

Holy fuck. Was that her?

It had to be. I'd know that skirt and those legs anywhere.

My cock tightened, and I adjusted myself in my seat, my mind churning.

This dude everyone called Spider sat down next to her, and she smiled up at him.

Oh. They must be a couple. And why did I feel disappointed?

Then another girl—this one a blonde—sat on the other side of him, making me wonder which he was banging. Because he started talking to both of them, even going so far as to wrap an arm around each of their chairs. But his attention seemed more on Ballet Girl. Huh. Was the dancer seeing the notorious English kid who had a rep as a hothead?

It didn't fit with what I had in my head. And it pissed me off.

Surprising myself, I scooted my chair over, trying to get a look at her profile. Because what if I'd been sitting next to her every day for the past two months in Calculus or wherever and hadn't even known it?

"Dude, you're right on top of me." Zero sent me a questioning look as I leaned over in his space.

I moved back to my side. Feeling off.

Why did I care what she looked like?

"Just trying to see the speaker," I muttered, since the

assembly had already started.

Zero stood. "Dude, if it's that important to you, let's switch, then."

I jumped on it, getting up and letting him have my seat. I settled back in the hard chair and let my eyes eat her up.

I had a great view. Her dark hair was scrapped back in a tight bun, giving me full access to her soft profile. The first thing I noticed right away was the curve of her lips and how full they were. I wondered if her mouth was always that pink or if she wore lipstick. Her skin was milky white with high cheekbones and a straight nose. I didn't see what color her eyes were, but her lashes were incredibly long and black.

She smiled at something, and I lost my breath. Just a little. She wasn't beautiful or made-up like some of the girls here. At all. But, she was lovely to look at, delicate yet with a strong body that she'd obviously worked on for years. She laughed again, and just the sound of it mesmerized me. Maybe because within her laugh, I detected a unique quality about her, something I didn't have. She seemed hopeful and optimistic, like she believed in fairytales and butterflies and shit.

Yeah, stay away from that.

I avoided Mary Poppins type girls.

But then why did I find myself leaning forward, just a little closer. Dying to see the color of those eyes. Needing to see her face up close.

Someone sat on the other side of me, coming in late to the assembly.

I glanced over to see Nora Blakely, resident BA genius, National Belltone Spelling Bee Champion, and all around odd person. We didn't talk much, but we'd grown up together here in Highland Park. And I liked her.

I nudged my head toward Ballet Girl and whispered, "Nora, who's that girl?"

She arched a brow at me, and I played it up and grinned. "I mean, you're gorgeous, of course, but just trying to place if I know her."

She smirked, and I don't think she cared one way or the other about who I was interested in. After a few minutes of looking at Ballet Girl, she turned to me. "Pretty sure her name is Dovey. I think she's a scholarship student. Maybe from Ratcliffe."

My mind raced. Dovey? Like the bird? And Ratcliffe? God, what a hell hole.

"Is she seeing Spider?" I felt silly with the hushed voices, but I didn't want Ballet Girl to hear us. Because that would be weird.

She raked her eyes over the three of them in her wacky analytical way that most of us had gotten used to over the years. "Hmm. Not sure. His body is pivoted toward Dovey, and his eyes keep darting to her, like he's checking in on her. It seems like he really likes her. It's interesting." She paused. "But the other girl has her hand on his crotch, and he seems to like it, so yeah, I don't know what's going on there. Lots of mixed signals."

Well, that didn't help. But I had a name.

"Thanks," I said, straightening back up.

My phone pinged with a text from my mom.

You're on my mind. I love you, she said.

My heart dipped and from within, I got a burst of hope. The speaker and the gym zoomed away, making me forget about Dovey and if she had a boyfriend. Instead, I focused on my mom. It had been months since she'd texted me.

Did this mean she was finally moving on?

Was she ready to forgive me?

Love you too, I typed out. And of course I wanted to type more, like ask her if she'd come to my game this week or if she'd hang out with me and Dad tonight. Maybe she'd cook us some fried yucca, a Brazilian dish a lot like French fries.

But I didn't ask those things because I didn't want to push her. If a text was all she could do, I'd take it.

I went home that afternoon feeling unsure about seeing Mom but still happy about the text she'd sent me. And I wanted to tell her my big news. A local television station was coming out to interview the team at our home game against Copeland Private, one of our biggest rivals. And even though I was a junior, the team had voted me to be the spokesperson. Maybe if she could just see how much they respected me, then maybe she would too.

But when I got home from practice, Mother wasn't waiting for me like I'd built up in my head. She wasn't downstairs, and when I got upstairs her bedroom door was shut.

I knocked. "Mom, you in there? I—I got your text. I love you, too."

I waited, my hands clenched.

Shuffling sounds filtered through the door. "I'm here," she said, the finality in her voice obvious. Like this was the last place in the world she wanted to be.

Frustration rose. Something had obviously happened between the text at school and me getting home. I sighed. I didn't understand her sickness, the prison that was her depression.

"Are you coming out, then?" I asked. *Please.*

Silence and then, "No. I—I just want to be alone."

Oh.

I got worried.

"Mom, please don't do anything stupid," I begged through the wood, my voice gentle.

"I'm not. I'm fine. Just go," her small voice said, the desolate sound in it breaking me into tiny pieces. Making me feel paper thin.

"Will you open the door a little? I want to see you," I said. Because if I could just *see* her, then I wouldn't worry.

She cracked the door, giving me a sliver of her beautiful face. She still had her pajamas on, but she'd combed her hair and showered. That was a big step. I smiled.

"See. All is well. Now go do your homework." Then very gently, she shut the door.

And from behind the door, I heard her crying softly.

Dammit.

I pressed my forehead to the door and fought my own emotion, feeling myself sinking into a bottomless pit, falling further and further. Defeat built in me, and I wanted to scream at her. I wanted to tell her to be strong and get over it and learn to live again and be a fucking mother to me, but none of those words spilled out of my mouth.

Because how could I ask her to be better when I felt so weak myself.

Fuck, fuck, fuck.

I'd done this to our family.

After a while, I gave up on her opening the door. I shook off the darkness and drove the Porsche straight to Marissa's apartment. An older girl who'd graduated from

BA two years earlier, she was a dependable hook-up. Rich and vivacious, she knew exactly how to blow my mind. Among other things.

Loud music blared from outside the door but went quiet when I knocked.

She opened it, her eyes skating over my track pants and wife-beater. I leaned against the door jam and eased off my Ray Bans, cocking an eyebrow at her skimpy shorts and halter top, my eyes lingering on her ample tits. *That* was what I needed.

I grinned, turning on the charm. “Hello, Beautiful.”

She huffed, flicking a piece of blonde hair over her shoulder. “You didn’t call. You think I’m just sitting here waiting on you?”

“You want me to leave?” I murmured, biting my lip. Putting on a show for her.

She shivered, her eyes dilating, probably remembering the raunchy things we’d done in this apartment. In the kitchen, in the bathroom, in the bedroom, on the patio. Marissa was wild, and I ate that up.

She pouted at me with red lips. “You can come in, but you’d better be good to me.”

I didn’t know about being good to her, but I could sure as hell make her feel good.

I walked in and she shut the door.

“You’ve never had better,” I said, pushing her up against the den wall and framing her face with my hands. She gazed up at me in what looked a little like adoration, which slowed me down for a second, because I didn’t want any touchy-feely emotions involved in this.

I paused, leveling her with my gaze. “Hey, we’re just having fun, right?”

She swallowed. "Yeah, sure. No strings, baby."

Good. I kissed her long and hard until we were both panting and ready for more.

"Let's go to the bedroom," she whispered, wrapping her arms snakelike around my neck.

I cupped her breasts and squeezed, tweaking the nipples through her tight shirt.

"No, babe, right here. Going to make you come," I promised. Because I didn't want to wait. I wanted this ache gone, and I didn't mean the one in my pants.

Bending over, I sucked on her tits through her shirt, making her gasp and clutch me tighter. We kissed for a while, both of our hands rushing to get the other undressed. Forgetting the ghost of my mother, I pushed everything out of my head except for sex. And that got really easy when she fell to her knees and took me in her mouth while I watched, absently and with little attachment. She could have been any of the girls I'd been with in the past two years.

Being with her required no emotional investment.

Which was the safest thing with me.

After a few minutes of her going down on me, I picked her up, wrapped her legs around my waist, and took her against the wall. I grabbed her hips, tossed my head back, and before I could stop it, Dovey came to mind.

It slowed me down for a sec, and I tried to push her out … because what the hell was I doing daydreaming over some random girl who didn't matter when I had this hot older girl?

But she wouldn't get out of my head.

Fuck it.

I gave in and went with it, imagining Dovey pinned

against the wall, her legs imprisoning me. Yeah. So. Fucking. Good. I grunted and went with it, slamming into Marissa, but wanting another.

And it was wrong, so wrong of me, but I played my fantasy in my head again, of Dovey dancing for me, of her being in love with me, of her needing me with all my rough spots and flaws, and lastly, I visualized *me* loving her in return.

But then my dream took on another angle, sweeter almost, as I imagined me and Dovey at my lake house in White Rock. I made a bed for us out of quilts and pillows under the night sky, under the stars and moon. I made love to her again, this time gazing intently at her face to face. Because now I knew what she looked like.

I told her I'd love her forever.

And I don't even know why.

"Love swallows up all the good parts,
but ballet gives it all back."
–Dovey

SEPTEMBER DRIFTED INTO October.

I continued working on my performance pieces with Jacques. He kept asking me out, but I always said no. I mean, he was hot with his big muscles and French accent, but I knew I had to keep my distance. The loneliness ate at me, but I kept remembering my mother and how love had ultimately destroyed her.

I didn't want that for me.

I was surprised Spider continued dating Becca. I began to wonder if maybe he'd finally fallen for someone. Nah. I laughed. Spider was just bidding his time until the next cute girl came along.

The first time I'd met him had been freshman year, and I hadn't been impressed with him. Sure he was handsome and popular—with a hot English accent—but he'd had a rep as a trouble maker.

It had all began one day in art class when he'd looked across the row of space that separated our work areas and poked fun at my dandelion still life. In retrospect, my painting had been awful, but I didn't need some smart-ass, cocky guy telling me. So after class, I'd followed him to his locker, determined to let him know he couldn't trash talk me. I was only fourteen at the time, but being from Ratcliffe, I had a chip on my shoulders, and I was determined to not take his shit.

I'd eyed his tattoo and said, "Spider is a weird name. Did you know that spiders are almost all homosexual? The females rule and prefer each other, and the males are an afterthought. That's also why the black widow kills the male after mating, because she views him as a genetic sacrifice. Not to mention, he's a wimp, all weak and scared. He's good enough to be her protein though. *Yummmy*," I said, rubbing my belly.

He smirked. "Are you saying I'm gay?"

"Don't care one way or the other. Lots of my friends are gay. The point is I may be a girl, but like the black widow, I will kick your ass if you ever make fun of me again." Total bluff. I gave him a bright smile and turned to leave. "Cheerio, mate."

He followed me. "How do you know so much about spiders?"

I gave him a haughty look. "Duh. I read."

He lightly touched his tat. "So it's true, then?"

"No. Yes. I don't know. Maybe the black widow lets the male live sometimes. If he brings her a tasty insect probably. Because females like to eat." Yeah.

He blinked. "No. Are spiders gay?"

I tapped my chin, hiding my glee at his distress.

"Meh, I made it up mostly. Just to get your attention and make a point." And then I added, "It's called hyperbole. Or a lie. Whatever."

He'd smiled, his eyes crinkling and a dimple popping out on his cheeks.

I'd grinned back. *He liked me.* And there you go. I had a friend. "And by the way, your banana still life? It looked like a penis. So don't give me grief for some dandelions."

He'd barked out a laugh. "Yeah, the banana was *hard* to get right."

And that had been the beginning of mine and Spider's friendship.

The bell rang in algebra, pulling me from my memories. I rose up out of my desk and left, headed for lunch.

I turned the corner to go into the cafeteria when a tall guy with dark hair came out of the library, a pretty girl on each arm. Emma Easton and April Novak were the girls, mean ones if you listened to gossip, and each bookended Cuba Hudson, one of the most—no, wait, *the most* popular guy at BA.

I took him in, unabashedly, since Spider wasn't here like he usually was, offering his critiques of the guys I thought were hot. There was no doubt, Cuba was the most beautiful guys I'd ever seen. Yeah, yeah, I know beautiful is a weird word for a guy, but when it fits, it just does. With a lethal kind of aura, he positively oozed sex, pulling your gaze into his magnetic vortex. The fitness side of me admired his physique with analytical eyes, ghosting over the broad chest and bunched muscles. But most of all, the dreamer in me got chills at his golden-yellow eyes, just like what I imagined an exotic jungle cat would have. I'd meet his gaze once or twice over the years and had shivered each time. With anticipation or heat—or dread? No idea. But his eyes did cause some kind of weird visceral reaction in me like no other, almost as if we shared a connection, like we were kindred spirits—

Gah. I sounded completely stupid. Cuba Hudson had no idea who I was, nor did he give a shit about meeting my eyes. No one here did. Well, except for Spider.

I tore my eyes from his form—thank goodness he hadn't noticed me staring.

I walked into lunch and when I didn't see Spider, I figured he was out on the quad with Becca. I sat by myself to eat.

Being alone in a room full of people who never really looked at you didn't bother me.

Or at least that's what I told myself.

CUBA

"When you see the things I have, you grow up fast."
–Cuba

OUR BIG GAME arrived in early November. I had the best night of my career, sacking the Copeland quarterback four times in the first quarter as scouts from ESPN watched in the stands. In the end, we stomped them, the final score 21 to 3. It looked like BA was headed to the regional championships.

I came off the field after the television interview was over, and Dad met me at the gate, a huge smile on his face. "Son, damn proud of you and that game. Congrats on the win." He pulled me in for a hug. I sank into it, needing the contact.

"You deserve all the happiness in the world, you know that right?" he said.

I didn't deserve shit.

I asked him the most important question. "Did Mom come?"

He twisted his lips, his eyes darting around everywhere but landing on nothing. "Nah, she was tired. She said to tell you good luck." Yeah. I wondered if that was true or if he was just saying that to make me feel better.

I nodded, ignoring the lump in my throat.

Zero yelled at me as he ran over to us. "Dude, party in the field tonight. You in? The whole team's coming." The field was an area back behind Zero's house where we went to hang out and drink after games. His parents didn't care as long as we didn't make a bonfire. But we could crank the music up as loud as we wanted.

"Go on and have fun with your team, Cuba," Dad said, giving me a pat. "You should celebrate your win. I'm headed to a late dinner in Dallas anyway."

"Who's watching mom?" I snapped, angry with him for always having somewhere to go. His running around for work never ended with him. Yeah, he owned a sports team, but fuck it, he had a family too, and maybe he needed to wake up and see that Mother was—

"The sitting service. They came over before the game and should be there until around midnight. Don't worry about her, okay? She's getting help, seeing a new doctor. Maybe we'll see some improvement. You gotta live your life."

What? Live my life when my mother obviously wasn't?

I said, "Yeah, sounds good. I'll see you in the morning."

He nodded and walked away, and don't think that I didn't miss that his shoulders were hunched over. My anger with him immediately faded because he was in pain too. Like me, he recognized our lives were slowly unraveling day by day. And we were helpless to do anything about it except watch.

And so the night went.

I drove to that party, got trashed on Jack and ended up banging some ditzy cheerleader in the front seat of my Porsche. It wasn't even good sex, and I kept calling her by the wrong name. During most of it, I imagined myself outside my body, watching what occurred, assessing the level I'd sunk to. I didn't like what I'd become, but here's the thing, I didn't want to stop either. Because I'd do anything to make the memories get the fuck out of my head.

I'm a no-good useless bastard.

CUBA

"Could she cast away darkness?"
–Cuba

AT THE END of November we lost our play-off game to a school in Austin. I dealt with it like I did everything else. I worked out more, swam more, fucked more. And I studied. Because I had my goal of rectifying myself by helping others, and I wasn't going to let go of that.

Christmas arrived on a cold morning. I came downstairs with dad, both of us shocked to find Mother in the kitchen, dressed in a classy outfit and wearing make-up.

I stood transfixed. It had been a nearly a year since I'd seen her looking like she used to when she'd be heading out for some charity or a school board meeting.

She waved a can of cinnamon rolls in front of me. "Good morning. You wanna eat before we open gifts?" She smiled, the effort seeming to come from deep within her.

I swallowed, finding my voice. "Mom?"

She fidgeted. Looking unsure and fragile.

I moved toward her like a man possessed and swept her up in my arms, swinging her around. She laughed, and I buried my face in her neck, inhaling her clean scent. My throat got clogged as she clutched me back, her small hands holding on to me like her life depended on it.

God, she was better.

After a quick breakfast together, we went into the den and opened gifts. I'd gotten them both books from their favorite authors, and they'd gotten me a new television for my room. Later that evening, we ate turkey and all the fixings along with some of my mom's traditional Brazilian favorites. She put her apron on and got to work, banging and clanging around the kitchen. It sounded like heaven.

After dinner, we sat around the fire in Dad's study, listening to Christmas music and talking, catching her up on all the latest gossip about the Mavericks and our Highland Park friends. All in all, it was one of the best days I'd ever had. Maybe because my hope came roaring back. And there's nothing like being as low as you can get and then getting that spark that tells you it's not over yet, that you still have fight left in you.

Yeah.

And the only thing I could think in my head was that she was back, she was back, she was back.

But she wasn't.

CUBA

"Money hides a world of pain."
–Cuba

JANUARY MEANT A new semester at BA. It also meant a change in classes since we were on the block schedule.

So after the holiday break, I walked into my new World History class, checking out the other students, wondering who I would be getting to know for the next few months.

I came to an abrupt halt when I saw Dovey in the front row.

Sure, I'd seen her around the school some. I'd catch glimpses of her in the cafeteria or the library, but I never allowed myself to look too long or linger over her attributes.

I don't even know how to explain my natural avoidance of her except to say that I sensed she was different. From the way she'd danced, I'd gotten the vibe of someone driven and strong and perhaps pure. Crazy to get all that from watching her, but the emotion in her had been beautiful.

Hell, I'd taken a hit because of it.

I didn't want to mess with that quality about her. Because I would screw her up like I do everything else. The bottom line was she wasn't like any of the girls here, and my heart told me to stay away. I only wanted to fuck, not get close to someone. And never in a million years did I want to fall in love with anyone, and I sensed—based on my ridiculous dreams—she might make me fall.

So yeah, I told myself to keep walking by her desk. And with Herculean effort, I did. I went and sat next to Zero, who also had his eyes on Dovey.

"Who is that?" he asked me, leaning over and whispering out of the corner of his mouth.

"No one," I said. "Some chick from the projects. I wouldn't waste my time if I were you."

He scoffed, pushing auburn hair off his face. "Fucking body to die for. And did you see her ass in those yoga pants? It might be worth it to slum with her."

I glared at him, my heart pounding loud and for no apparent reason. I sucked in a sharp breath, trying to get it under control.

What the hell was wrong with me?

Why did the thought of Zero with Dovey make me want to punch his lights out?

I pointed over at Emma Easton. "Now that's the girl you need. And she just broke up with Matt."

He rolled his eyes at me. Ha. We both knew they'd be back together by the end of the week.

And then class started.

I opened my book as the teacher started in with a lecture on the Roman Empire, but my eyes took in Dovey, assessing what it was about her that got to me. Finally after a few minutes, I decided she was plain and not my type at all.

Then it happened.

She turned around to pick up a piece of paper the teacher was sending around for us to sign. My world … my fucking life … altered when her eyes connected with mine for what seemed like a long time, but it only had to be a few seconds. They were blue. A peacock blue with hints of green.

She would never be plain.

She smiled, just a tiny one, kinda like the smile you'd give to any human who you happened to make eye contact with by accident.

I blushed. I have no idea why. Maybe because I'd imagined fucking her in every position that was anatomically feasible.

Flustered, I looked down at my desk, fiddling with my notebook, feeling confused and self-conscious. *Me.* The guy who could have any girl he wanted was freaking out over some girl who didn't even register on the who's who of BA.

When I glanced back up, she'd already turned back around.

I didn't hear a thing the professor said that day, my eyes on Dovey, picturing me and her together. Falling in love.

So stupid.

Because falling for a girl like her was a terrible idea.

As soon as the bell rang, I bolted from my seat for my next class.

When the following day rolled around, I took a seat

far, far away from her. No reason. Just thought maybe I needed a change of scenery is all.

LATER THAT WEEK, I walked in our house after a post-season workout at the gym. Mom had texted earlier, checking to make sure I was on schedule to arrive on time. She'd specifically asked if I'd be home by four o'clock, and her reaching out sent alarm bells off in my head. It was odd. Why did she care what time I came home? Unless …

She was fine, I kept telling myself.

Yet, I'd made sure to be home.

I didn't see her in the den or the kitchen or outside by the pool, where she liked to hang out sometimes and read. With queasy flutters in my stomach, I made my way upstairs. I knocked on her locked door, but got nothing. I pulled my phone out and called her. Sure enough I could hear it ringing in the background inside her bedroom.

"Mother, are you in there?" I yelled into the wood.

Nothing but silence.

"Open the door, please," I begged her, my ear pressed tight against the door, aching to hear at least a sniffle or something from her. Nada.

My stress level skyrocketed. She *always* answered me when I knocked.

I banged again and got nothing but an empty silence.

"Dammit, I'm coming in there," I called out, ramming my shoulder into the door. It thudded, loosening a little but not opening. I grabbed a credit card from my wallet, my gut screaming at me to *get to her, get to her, get to her*.

Finally, after some jiggling, the credit card popped the lock, and I rushed in.

She wasn't in bed, so I ran to the bathroom, coming to an abrupt halt, a dawning sense of horror growing in me at what I saw.

My mother, her honey-colored skin pale, lay nude in a bathtub full of water, blood oozing from her slit wrists.

Fuck me.

I yelled until my throat gave out, running to her and pulling her out of the water and into my arms. Craziness hit me, making me forget every first aid class I'd ever taken.

"Please don't leave me," I choked out, my adrenaline finally kicking in. I grabbed towels from the nearby shelving and pressed them to her wrists, applying pressure.

"Mary-Carmen," I shouted in her face, using her given name, praying her eyes opened. My fingers found a faint pulse on her neck.

"Thank God," I whispered, sitting her on the marble tiled floor so I could pull out my phone.

I called 911.

Sixteen agonizing minutes later, I watched the paramedics wrap her wrists and then strap her in a gurney they'd put in her bedroom. One of them had an oxygen mask on her.

"Is she going to be okay?" I asked, clutching my stomach, holding in the nausea that I couldn't let out, because I had to keep my shit together. For her.

No one answered me.

My nerves broke, and I rushed for the bathroom, puking my guts out in the red-smeared bathroom. I closed my eyes, wishing Dad was here and not out of town. I'd called him while they worked on her, and he'd left immediately on the private jet the Mavericks owned.

Later in the hospital as I sat by her bed, I gazed into her face, self-loathing eating me inside, tearing me down. Her destruction had begun with me. I lay my head by hers and … shit … I fucking cried, hating myself.

A WEEK LATER, my mom agreed to check into a treatment facility for depression. Thankfully, she'd cut herself horizontally and not vertically, missing her vital arties. From her hospital bed, she'd promised us it was a mistake. That she hadn't meant to go so far. Dad got her another new therapist. I just felt numb.

And perhaps that is why on the day I went back to school, my feet automatically went to the one place I'd been denying them: straight to the desk behind Dovey in history class.

I sat down, my eyes entranced by the way her hair fell down from her high ponytail. I wanted to wrap my hand in it and tug on it until she turned around. I wanted her to face me so I could—

Well, shit, I didn't know why I wanted her to face me.

She moved, getting a book out of her backpack, the simple motion causing the air to stir and giving me my first scent of Dovey. She smelled sweet with a hint of spice about her, like the wild flowers that grew at our lake house in White Rock.

I stared at her so long and hard, I wondered if she could feel my gaze. Could she feel my intensity? Did she sense that her lightness was the perfect foil for my darkness?

When the bell rang and she stood, I did too. I opened my mouth to say … hell, I have no idea what I was going to say … but I didn't. I was nervous and jittery, my confidence shot.

She flicked her eyes at me, seemingly not interested.

"I'm Cuba," I said to her in a rush. She'd been turning to go, but paused and looked back at me.

She blinked up at me, blushed, and then smiled. "Dovey," she said, hitching her book bag up on her shoulder.

We stood there and she gave me an expectant look, and I fidgeted, realizing it was my turn to talk.

But I had nothing. The guy who'd been with so many girls I'd lost count; the guy who didn't care about love or relationships or all that mushy stuff. I just stood there like a total idiot. And because I felt panic rising, I ducked my head and walked around her. Pretty much snubbing her. God, I'm an ass. I had no clue how to treat a nice girl.

CUBA

"Dream bigger than your fears."
–Cuba

THE NEXT DAY, I walked in the cafeteria for lunch, and Dovey was the first thing I saw, sitting alone at one of round tables in the back.

I stopped and stared, remembering a sickeningly sweet dream I'd had the night before about her. *How could I get this girl out of my head?*

Maybe I just needed to go for it with her.

I mean, it was obvious I had a thing for her. And fuck it—I was tired of running from my feelings. Maybe, just maybe this one time, I could be responsible and really just … put someone else first.

With clammy hands and sweat popping out, I walked to her. She didn't even notice me as I stood right in front of her. Maybe this wasn't a good idea. I'd only screw it up in the end.

Yet …

Did I want to wonder about what might have been?

Life doesn't give you do-overs. Luke Skywalker didn't get one when he blew up the Death Star. He'd had one shot, and he'd nailed it.

Yeah.

I took a deep breath and sat down directly across from her.

"I had a dream about you. A good one," I said, right as she took a giant bite from what I think was a peanut butter sandwich. A glob of strawberry jam slid out of the corner of her mouth, and she wiped it off and looked up. To be honest, she kinda glared at me.

"Yeah? Is that so?" she said, arching a brow.

I nodded.

She talked around her chews. "What's the joke? Did Spider put you up to this?"

What? Why would Spider put me up to something? I didn't even like that asshole.

I shrugged. "No joke. I dreamed about you."

"Do tell," she said, eyeing my black knit shirt, her gaze lingering over my chest. Some of my confidence came back. Thank God. I was starting to wonder where the hell my balls were.

I leaned in. "You may not know this, but my mother's a gypsy. She tells me what my dreams mean."

"Really?" she said. "I thought your mother was Brazilian. Aren't gypsies Romanian?"

"My father's side is Romanian."

"Nope." She packed her lunch up. "Your dad is Archie Hudson, owner of the Dallas Mavericks, and as American as apple pie."

"True. But I did have a dream about you."

She made a scoffing sound. "Hello, I've been here

since freshman year, and this is the first time you've noticed me? Face it, I'm not part of your little group over there." She pointed out the cheerleaders and jocks at a table in the back. "Not buying it."

Then she got out her math homework and ran a quick finger down the page like she was checking over it.

She was ignoring *me*. When most girls would have be falling all over me.

"So what clique do you belong to?" I asked, eyeing the empty seats around her.

"The non-conformist one. I don't fit in with the Goths or the geeks or the choir people or the skaters or the druggies. You get the picture. I like being alone." She shifted her body out of the chair and stood. "Now, if you'll excuse me, I have a math class to get to."

I stood too. "Wait."

"Why?"

"You didn't ask about the dream. Don't you want to know?" And then out of nowhere, I felt myself blushing, and she saw it too, because she went still, taking in my fire-engine-red face.

After one more searching glance, she settled back on the hard chair. "Dream, huh."

I sat back down. "And by the way, I've noticed you even before our class this year. You're different." My voice went low. "And I saw you dance."

"When?"

"Back in the fall. The football field has a clear view into the windows of the Symthe Dance building. You have ballet practice there every day from two to five, and I had practice at three. It was bound to happen."

She crossed her arms, but I saw a glint of something

in her eye, as if I'd intrigued her. "Did you like what you saw?"

"I got tackled by a lineman called Tank while I stood there watching you. He hit me so hard, I had to go to the doctor and get checked out."

Her mouth parted. "Because you were so enamored with seeing me dance?" she said.

"Yep."

She grinned. "Maybe you still have that concussion."

"My head is clear as a bell, Dovey." I winked at her, relaxing for the first time since I'd sat down. She was funny, and I liked how she was kinda distrustful of me. Because it meant she was smart too. And sexy. And her eyes were the most beautiful color of blue. And her skin was silky and pale, unlike my own darker complexion.

Her full lips curved up in a little smile, and right then, I wanted my hands on her. I ran my eyes over her grey tunic, imagining her tits and how small they'd be, yet they'd fit perfectly in the palm of my hand. I bet her nipples were red and if I sucked on them—

She sighed. "Okay, I'm curious. Tell me about this dream."

I cleared my throat, picking through the memories. "It started out with you in this blue dress, cut down to here," I murmured, grazing my hands down to my stomach. Yeah, I loved low-cut.

"Blue isn't my color. I'm more of a black girl. Sometimes grey."

I shrugged. In most my dreams she was naked. "Anyway, this dress had lace on it and … I don't know … stuff. And it matched your eyes, a deep blue like a stormy sea."

"You're very poetic," she said.

"Thank you," I said, my mouth twitching.

She chuckled, and fucking elation went through me.

"I made you laugh. I like it," I said.

"Okay, blue dress, very revealing. Is there more?" she asked, waving my hand.

"You had on these amazing heels. I don't remember the color … maybe an animal print … but I do remember they made you tall, your face almost level with mine." I rubbed my jaw. "I liked those shoes."

"Like these?" she stuck out her leg, showing me her plain flats.

My eyes ate up her legs, getting all kinds of turned on. I bit back a groan, picturing them wrapped around my waist. At this rate, I'd come in my pants.

"No, but I like those too," I murmured. "Your legs are long, Dovey. It's hot."

She straightened like she was leaving. "I don't think I like where your dream is headed."

Wait, don't …

"No, it wasn't like that. It was just you standing on these stone steps, maybe in front of a museum or a library. You were waiting for someone, and when I showed up you ran straight into my arms. Like we'd known each other forever. Like we were a couple." I glanced down at the table and then back at her. "And then I kissed you."

"Oh?"

"Yeah," I said.

"Tongue?"

"Most definitely," I murmured.

"Long? Short?"

I quirked an eyebrow. "Hot and deep. Languorous."

"Languorous? One of your SAT words?"

I grinned. "It means leisurely and unhurried. It fits."

She nibbled on her nails, her eyes on my lips. I licked mine, and her face went pink.

"Is that it? No nudity?" she said.

She totally sounded disappointed.

I put my elbows on the table, settling in. "Nope. Isn't it enough to be the most romantic kiss known to mankind? Incredible doesn't even touch it. The way your mouth fit to mine …" I broke from her eyes, blushing again.

When I got the nerve to look at her again, her attention was on my tat. Ah, did she like ink on guys? I crossed my arm, flexing my bicep a little so she'd have a better view of the twisting vine as it crossed my arms.

I imagined her mouth tracing those roses.

As if she read my mind, she turned pink when she looked up and met my gaze. I grinned.

Then the bell rang. Dammit. I didn't want this to be over.

She let out a sigh and stood. "This was fun, but I have class."

I rose and grabbed her backpack before she could. "I'll walk you."

She shrugged like *whatever* and we walked out of the cafeteria together and down the hall.

"This is me," she said, stopping at a classroom a few minutes later. I peeked in. Geometry. I suddenly wished I was in here with her.

I shook my head. That was ridiculous.

I handed her the backpack, our hands brushing, sending little shocks through my body.

And right there, I went for it. I hadn't officially asked

a girl out on a real date in months, but with her, I was making the exception.

"I bought two tickets to see *Les Miserables* in a few weeks. Primo seats. Wanna go?" I asked.

"Guys like you aren't part of my plan," she said.

"If that's a challenge, then I accept."

"No challenge, just the truth." She moved to walk away, but I pulled her back with my next words. Because I was feeling all kinds of insecure. "Okay, tell me straight. Are you just completely disinterested in me? You say one thing, but your body is saying something else."

"My body?" She looked annoyed, but I kept on.

"Yeah, I'm getting this vibe from you. Makes me want to ditch school and drag you out to the barn at the back of campus where we can be alone. Maybe it's all me, I don't know, but I think you feel it too."

"You really put yourself all out there, don't you?" she said, her eyes big.

"Maybe. If this is my only shot, I'm going for it." I paused. "Let me in, Dovey."

"Why me?"

I didn't know *why* her.

But I sensed this was my only chance to get her attention, so I did something crazy.

I leaned in to her and sang out in a low voice, "Why do birds sing? Why do phones ring? Why does my heart fly? For all I know, you'll make me cry. Why do fools fall in love? Why were you named after a dove?" I stopped and grinned, impressed with my spur of the moment performance.

Her mouth gaped. "That was the most atrocious thing I've ever heard."

"It was pretty cheesy, wasn't it?"

"Pure crap," she said, but then smiled.

I laughed, and I mean, *I laughed.* And the sound was so real and easy and good and she was just fucking perfect.

"Don't tell anyone I sing silly songs," I said teasingly. "Football players are supposed to be tough and mean."

She gave me a thoughtful look. "Everyone says you're pretty good on the field. That no quarterback is safe."

I didn't believe my own hype, actually. "Whatever."

"I hear you're the best defensive end BA has ever seen and a four-star recruit by ESPN."

I scratched an eyebrow. "Maybe." I leaned in closer. "Maybe you can come and watch me practice? I could use my own personal cheerleader in the stands."

"I thought the season was over anyway."

I shrugged. "I've got a recruiter coming to see me soon. Wanna be ready."

"Ah, well, I'm pretty busy." She paused, a weird look on her face. "But I'd love to see you in uniform."

My eyes widened. *Bingo!* "That can be arranged. Maybe you could wear your little ballet skirt?"

Visions of me slipping my hand up under her skirt flashed through my head. Again. Maybe she'd unlace my football pants, take my cock out and—fuck—I had to stop this line of thinking. Because, I think I really liked this girl, and something in me wanted to do right by her.

I wanted to woo her.

And that was the craziest thought I'd ever had.

I grinned at her red face. "Ah, I shouldn't have said that. You're thinking dirty thoughts."

"Am not," she said, but she didn't sound sure.

"Uh-huh." My lids lowered.

"How do you know?"

I leaned in. "I can read a girl. And based on the red face and dilated eyes, you like me."

Her breathing escalated, making me scoot in a tiny bit closer. I inhaled her wildflower scent, my heart beating like a drum.

"Get to know me, Dovey. Let's hang out. I promise I won't bite unless you want me to."

She let out a long sigh, like she was getting ready for a sermon. She said, "I appreciate your balls in coming up to me. I even applaud your whole 'I dreamed about you' line, because it was smooth. Just the right amount of humor with a touch of sexy. It's obvious you're a master at picking up girls. And the kissing part? That was excellent. Very subtle, and just enough to get my mind to thinking about us … you know … kissing." Her words faltered. "But at the end of the day, it won't work. We aren't compatible. We come from two different places. You're rich; I'm not. You like to party; I don't. You like high heels; I don't wear them. Good grief, your friends call you Hollywood. Then there's me. I work my ass off to get everything I have. So yeah, not feasible."

I straightened up. "I'll meet you after dance. I want to see you again before I go home."

She sputtered. "No. I just gave you a list of reasons why we can't go out."

"Yeah, I may have missed some of it. I was watching your mouth move," I murmured. "Got distracted by your lips."

"Is this a joke?" she asked.

"I don't play pranks." I waved at the space between

us. “We have a connection. I knew it the moment I sat down with you. You want to resist me, that’s fine. I like it. It’s like foreplay.”

I slid off my leather varsity jacket and wrapped it over her shoulders. “Meet me outside your building so you can give me my jacket back. That’s all. No more songs.”

I tweaked her nose. “And my dream was real.”

Her mouth opened and closed like a fish, making me chuckle. I gave her one last lingering look and turned and sauntered away. Totally pretending that I wasn’t a bundle of nerves.

Dovey

"Gypsies? Oh, he was good. Very good."
–Dovey

HOLY SHIZZLE. CUBA Hudson asked me out. What was the world coming to?

He slowly disappeared down the hall, headed to his own class. I watched until the other students swallowed him up and he was gone.

Why me?

"Bad juju," I murmured to no one is particular, stroking the supple texture of his coat. I made sure no one was looking and buried my face in the collar, inhaling his scent, sandalwood and musk. I wanted to wrap my whole body in it and roll around on the ground. I wanted to wave it around like a matador in front of all the snooty girls in my class. I wanted to take it home and sleep with it, maybe cuddle up to it like a teddy bear. Then I burst out laughing. *Craazzzy.*

Because a guy like him would never want a girl like

me.

At the end of classes, I hurried to the studio, changed, and lost myself in dance for the next three hours. I exercised and tried to forget about the sizzling way he'd looked at me. I tried to forget about how drop-dead gorgeous he was with those powerful arms and broad shoulders. I sure didn't think about his soft dark hair with red highlights from the sun or his intense yellow eyes. Or his hot as hell tattoo that I wanted to lick from beginning to end. Or the way he strolled around BA with his confident swagger, like what was between his legs was big and…

Stop!

Instead, I focused on his bad points and came up with two: his cockiness, which was off the charts insane, and then his reputation as a ladies' man. The gossip was he'd never had a serious girlfriend. He was a serial dater who tended to drop a girl when a better one came along. And even though these girls were often broken-hearted, they still considered him a friend. That takes skill and cunning, proving he was no dumb jock. A freaking genius was more like it, if you considered how he'd played me, how he'd seemed to know exactly what to say to reel me in.

He wasn't called the Heartbreaker of BA for nothing.

At five, I jerked a sweatshirt over my leotard and tights, not bothering to put my pants back on. There wasn't time. I stuck my feet in a pair of wooly boots and took off. He was probably out there right now, his eyes leveled at the door, waiting for me to exit. So, I avoided the front entrance and slipped out the side door and ran all the way to the parking lot, lugging my books, my dance bag, and his jacket. Several students gawked at me darting across the quad in my dance tights, but I didn't care.

His silver Porsche gleamed in the sunlight—of course everyone knew his car—its sleek lines screaming money and power. Just like Cuba. I stood there, pacing around, debating and thinking and berating myself for not immediately leaving. But it was hard because he'd sucked me in with his sweet talk and goofy song.

But, he had no idea *who* I really was.

And if he ever found out who my parents were, he'd drive out of here so fast all I'd have would be skid tracks on my heart.

And that thought sealed the deal.

I rose and draped his jacket over the driver's side mirror, somewhere he wouldn't miss it. And because I was tempted to linger there and wait for him, I ran all the way to my car.

I had ballet. That was enough.

CUBA

"It ain't over till I say it's over."
–Cuba

I WAITED FOR her for thirty minutes, until finally the dance instructor exited the building. I watched him lock up.

Apparently Dovey had slipped past me, probably leaving from a side door. Yeah, a girl dissing me was a first. And it sucked ass.

I shook my head as I walked back to my car. Maybe I'd come on too strong? Had the dream freaked her out? Should I have treated her like Marissa?

I reached my car and came to an abrupt halt, my eyes taking in the leather varsity jacket spread out on top of the driver's side mirror.

And I got it. She had liked me. That much had been obvious from the way she'd laughed at my song. But something was holding her back.

Maybe it was because we came from different worlds

like she said.

Maybe it was because of my bad rep with girls.

Maybe it was because she could see through my pretty exterior to the ugliness underneath.

But we weren't over. Hell no.

I drove home, and by the time I pulled up in my drive, I had the perfect plan to make her mine. To get her under me.

She'd have no idea what hit her.

Because this was just the beginning.

A very wicked beginning.

The End

Dear Reader,

The entire month of May, all proceeds from the sale of my prequel will benefit the Keith Milano Memorial Fund for Suicide Prevention which was established to help raise awareness about the devastating disease that is mental illness. Keith's spirit and laughter is kept alive through our efforts to increase awareness about mental illness and to raise money for education and imperative research. www.keithmilano.org

Also, thank you for reading my prequel and catching a glimpse into the world of the students from Highland Park, Texas, who attend Briarcrest Academy. Each novel is a standalone with a happily ever after. The first is *Very Bad Things*, my debut which hit #1 in the New Adult College Age category on Amazon. It was also voted as one of the top five romances of 2013 by A is for Alpha B is for Book. It was on twenty-two different top ten lists.

If you'd like the conclusion to Cuba and Dovey, their story continues in *Very Wicked Things*, a critically acclaimed full length novel, now available at all retailers.

Hearing from you is very important to me. Honestly, it makes my day. I love to talk about my characters like they are real people (they are in my head!), and I love to meet new people. So please drop me a line on my website or on Facebook.

Book reviews are like gold to indie writers, and you have no idea how we relish each one. If you have time, I'd appreciate and love an honest, heartfelt review from you.

Thank you for being part of my fictional world,

Ilsa Madden-Mills.

Now read the novel *Very Wicked Things*!
Now available at all retailers.

BRIARCREST ACADEMY SERIES
Reading Order:
Very Bad Things
Very Wicked Beginnings
Very Wicked Things

For more information about the next book, please visit my social media sites:

www.ilsamaddenmills.com

Facebook:
www.facebook.com/authorilsamaddenmills?ref=hl

Goodreads:
www.goodreads.com/author/show/7059622.Ilsa_Madden_Mills

ILSA MADDEN-MILLS WRITES about strong heroines and sexy alpha males that sometimes you just want to slap. She spends her days with two small kids, a neurotic cat, and her Viking husband. She collects magnets and rarely cooks except to bake her own pretzels. When she's not typing away at a story, you can find her drinking too much Diet Coke, jamming out to Pink, or checking on her carefully maintained chocolate stash. She loves to hear from fans and fellow authors. Drop her a line on her website or Facebook page.

I CAN'T CLOSE out this prequel without thanking my sweet editor Rachel Daven Skinner who donated her time and skills in editing. Like me, she became attached to Cuba and Dovey and wanted to be part of the charitable organization we are supporting. Also, I'd like to thank Julie Titus of JT Formatting. She is talented beyond compare, and she fit me in under the wire. Wahoo! Last but not least is Denise Milano Sprung, a wonderful blogger who shared her story with me about her brother and his struggle with depression. I never met Keith Milano, yet I *know* him… and his story resonates in my heart. Thank you, ladies. Much love to you all